National Library
of Australia

Questacon

National
Portrait
Gallery

High Court
of Australia

National Gallery of
Australia

Aboriginal
Tent Embassy

Museum of
Australian
Democracy

National
Electoral
Education
Centre

Old Parliament House

National
Archives
of Australia

Parliament House

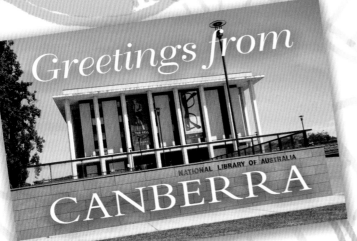
Greetings from
CANBERRA

NATIONAL LIBRARY OF AUSTRALIA

THE NATIONAL ARCHIVES

First published in 2022 by

 wild dog

PO Box 135
Fitzroy VIC 3065
Australia
wdog.com.au

Printed and bound in China by Everbest Printing Investment Limited

ISBN: 9781742036120

10 9 8 7 6 5 4 3 2 1   22 23 24 25 26

A catalogue record for this book is available from the National Library of Australia

NATIONAL LIBRARY OF AUSTRALIA

MIX
Paper from responsible sources
FSC® C124385
www.fsc.org

FSC® is a non-profit international organisation established to promote the responsible management of the world's forests.

For my sisters, Rosie and Giorgina. K.S.

For Sophie and Felix, who will change the world. C.W.

KRYS SACLIER is an electoral educator who has taught thousands of children from around Australia how to vote. Krys has written for television, radio and the press and is a qualified primary school teacher. She lives with her lovely family and a non-stop Burmese cat. Her first book with Wild Dog Books, *Vote for Me*, was also illustrated by Cathy Wilcox.

CATHY WILCOX has been drawing cartoons since she was old enough to scratch the furniture. She earned her letters at art college and was eventually taken in by the *Sydney Morning Herald*. There, she has churned out cartoons almost daily since 1989, pausing only to procreate, make cups of tea and collect cartooning awards.

Thank you to all the amazingly knowledgable people who work in educational tourism, and especially to the following folk who assisted with the research for this book:

Marissa Beard from the National Museum of Australia; Tyronne Bell from Thunderstone Aboriginal Cultural Services; Sally Cornish for information about the Museum of Australian Democracy; Karina Edwards from The High Court of Australia; Grant Fry from Government House; Michelle Hughes from the National Archives of Australia; Ben Pratten from the National Library of Australia; Jo Reid from the National Electoral Education Centre; Edy Syquer from the Royal Australian Mint; Heather Tregoning from the National Arboretum Canberra; Garry Watson from National Capital Educational Tourism Project.

CAMP CANBERRA

BY THE SMART AND EXCELLENT STUDENTS OF MOUNT MAYHEM PRIMARY SCHOOL

FARRELOSAURUS

Best Wishes
Krys Saclier

KRYS SACLIER

ILLUSTRATED BY

CATHY WILCOX

wild dog

ITINERARY

DAY 1

National Arboretum Canberra ● National Museum of Australia
National Archives of Australia ● Government House
National Gallery of Australia

DAY 2

Royal Australian Mint ● The High Court
National Capital Exhibition ● National Electoral Education Centre
Australian Parliament House ● Australian War Memorial

DAY 3

Australian Institute of Sport ● Australian Museum of Democracy
National Portrait Gallery ● National Library of Australia
Aboriginal Tent Embassy ● Questacon ● Mt Stromlo Observatory

GROUP 1: THE MENZIES – WITH MISS BARRIE

Farrel, Taylor, Aiko, Matthias, George, Leo

GROUP 2: THE GILLARDS – WITH MR TAM

Alexandria, Sean, Sophia, Areesha, Zain, Lillian

GROUP 3: THE HOLTS – WITH MS SPARKS

(KEEP AN EYE ON THESE KIDS)

Kira, Jack, Finn, Coen, Tilda, Maeve

ON THE BUS BY FARREL

It's scary-dark at six in the morning.

Ms Sparks has already given us a warning.

If she doesn't get her latté soon

Our trip to Canberra is gonna be doomed.

Yanni the bus driver saves the day.

He knows every café on the way.

Miss Barrie leads the singalong.

We all sing the song-words wrong.

It takes five hours before we see Telstra Tower.

Now we're in the capital city. It's so pretty.

Flags. Tulips. Roundabouts.

Jack's face is green! Check it out!

DAY 1 By the Menzies

FIRST STOP – THE NATIONAL ARBORETUM CANBERRA

An arboretum is like a zoo for trees. The National Arboretum has over 44,000 trees! Just like animals, some are endangered, so the arboretum is trying to save them by collecting and distributing their seeds.

My favourite tree was the Wollomi Pine. It was growing 200 million years ago. Everyone thought it was extinct, until hikers found some in the Blue Mountains. We saw something that would have been living when dinosaurs were stomping around. It's like touching the past.

Then we all rolled down the giant grassy hill before lunch.

Whee!

Let me tell ya what happen ...

Uncle Tarran Anderson, Wurundjeri elder, 2005

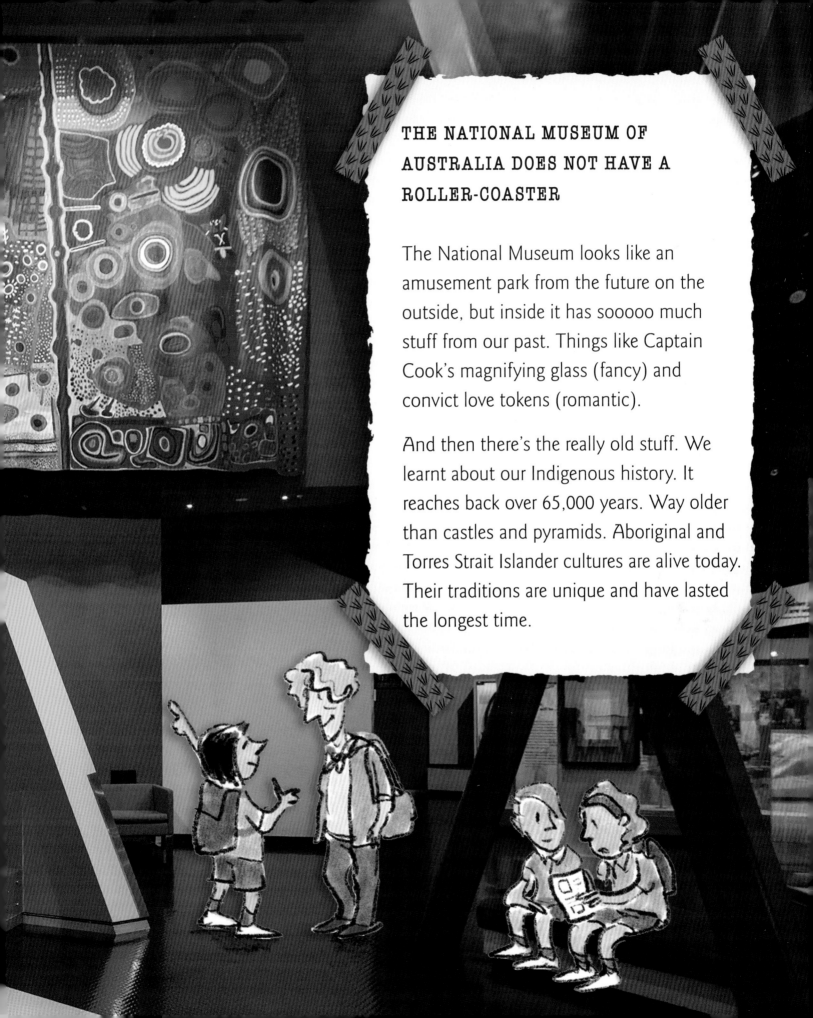

THE NATIONAL MUSEUM OF AUSTRALIA DOES NOT HAVE A ROLLER-COASTER

The National Museum looks like an amusement park from the future on the outside, but inside it has sooooo much stuff from our past. Things like Captain Cook's magnifying glass (fancy) and convict love tokens (romantic).

And then there's the really old stuff. We learnt about our Indigenous history. It reaches back over 65,000 years. Way older than castles and pyramids. Aboriginal and Torres Strait Islander cultures are alive today. Their traditions are unique and have lasted the longest time.

THE SECRET CABINET AT THE NATIONAL ARCHIVES OF AUSTRALIA

• The National Archives has all kinds of important documents and photos.

• The Australian Constitution is an important document because it has the rules for how our government should work. It was adopted in 1901, the year of Federation.

• The National Archives has the original Constitution hidden in a special case next to Queen Victoria's seal. Only special visitors like the students of Mount Mayhem Primary can see it.

• Queen Victoria was a famous ruler of England. She had to sign off on the Constitution because between 1788 and 1900, Australia was made up of colonies of Britain.

• Australia is a constitutional monarchy, which means we still have a queen or a king from England, but the Governor-General represents them here in Australia.

THE ROAD TO GOVERNMENT HOUSE

Yanni drove the bus down a long winding road to the Governor-General's beautiful house by the lake. Yanni told us that this is the road someone takes before they become the Prime Minister. We all felt very important.

Sadly, the Governor-General wasn't there. The Governor-General is always busy because they are our Head of State and have important duties. They can dissolve Parliament and issue writs for elections. Miss Barrie said the Governor-General gives out special awards called the Order of Australia Medal to outstanding Australians. Miss Barrie's nan has one because she raises money for charity.

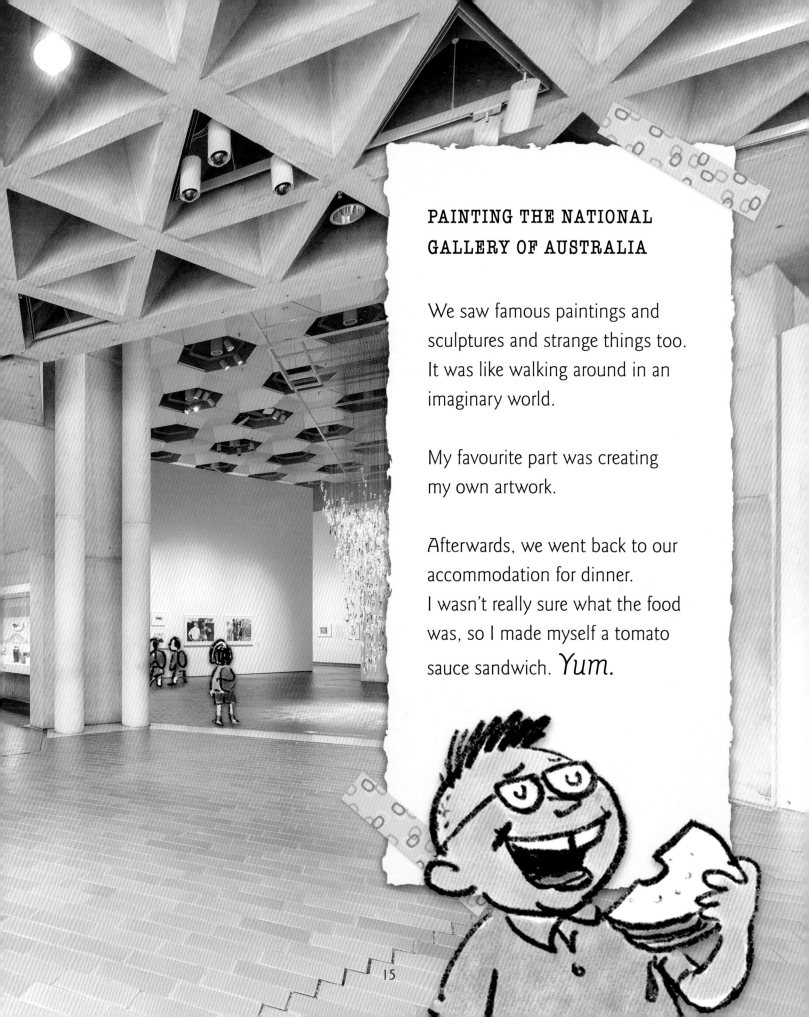

PAINTING THE NATIONAL GALLERY OF AUSTRALIA

We saw famous paintings and sculptures and strange things too. It was like walking around in an imaginary world.

My favourite part was creating my own artwork.

Afterwards, we went back to our accommodation for dinner. I wasn't really sure what the food was, so I made myself a tomato sauce sandwich. *Yum*.

DAY 2 By the Gillards

MAKING MONEY AT THE ROYAL AUSTRALIAN MINT

We stood above the factory and watched a robot called Titan lift a giant barrel of coins and pour them onto a production line. It sounded like thousands of cutlery drawers exploding.

Farrel asked if we could take a barrel of money home for a souvenir. Our guide said we could make our own dollar coin instead.

HISTORY FACT: The colonies of Australia didn't make their own currency until after the Gold Rush. Before then they used coins from other countries.

How do you plead?

Not guilty!

THE HIGH COURT OF AUSTRALIA IS THE HIGHEST COURT

Even though laws are made and changed in Parliament, we have courts to carry out the laws.

The High Court makes sure that the laws made in Parliament don't break any rules in the Constitution and that people's rights are protected. The judges in the High Court are independent. This is important for the 'separation of powers'. It means that the Parliament doesn't have all the power.

You can tell the High Court is important because the building is massive, with glass and concrete. Ms Sparks called it 'imposing'.

HIGH COURT of AUSTRALIA

YUMA TO THE NATIONAL CAPITAL EXHIBITION

Canberra is Australia's capital because no one could decide between Sydney and Melbourne, so they picked a spot in between.

In 1912, there was a big international competition to design the city, sort of like an old-time reality show. Walter Burley Griffin, an American architect, won. He worked on the design with his wife, Marion Mahoney Griffin.

We saw the original designs. They had a lake and lots of curved streets, which is probably why Jack keeps getting carsick.

The word Canberra means 'meeting place' in the local Ngunawal language, because different groups of Indigenous people would meet there to feast on migrating bogong moths. Our educator said the moths taste like peanut butter.

MORE NGUNAWAL WORDS
Hello – *Yuma*
Farewell (Safe Journey) – *Ngolyin*
Quick – *Baray*
Strong – *Yurwan*
Play – *Wagabaliri*

Alexandria is baray and yurwan – Alexandria is *quick* and *strong*.

NATIONAL ELECTORAL EDUCATION CENTRE

Taylor thought we were going to learn about electricity, but we really learnt about elections, although Ms Sparks said that voting is electrifying.

When we turn 18, we will have to vote in elections for the three levels of government: local, state and federal.

At federal elections, you have to vote for the House of Representatives and the Senate.

It's important that elections are fair and that everyone who can vote gets a chance to have their say. The Australian Electoral Commission has lots of ways for people to vote – even if they are in Antarctica.

We did a role play of an election and Miss Barrie chose me to be the ballot box guard because she said I'm the toughest person in the class. Afterwards, we had lunch in the Rose Gardens next door to Old Parliament House. Yanni cooked us democra-sausages on the barbecue.

Voting tastes **SO** good!

A TALE OF TWO HOUSES IN AUSTRALIAN PARLIAMENT HOUSE

THE HOUSE OF REPRESENTATIVES

Its colour is green.

Representatives are called Members of Parliament or MPs.

MPs represent their electorate. Australia is divided up into electorates – they might be different sizes but they have a similar population of voters.

We watched MPs in the House of Representatives during question time. They were all sitting in a big horseshoe shape. The government sits on one side and the opposition sits on the other. The government is the party that won at the last election. They win by having a majority of the elected MPs belonging to their party.

The prime minister (my future job) is the leader of the winning party.

Because the government has the majority, that makes it easy for them to pass bills – which are laws – through the House of Representatives.

THE SENATE

Its colour is red.

Members are called Senators.

Senators represent their state or territory.

The government still needs their bills to pass through the Senate, which isn't so easy because the government may not always have a majority in this house.

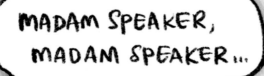

MADAM SPEAKER, MADAM SPEAKER...

ORDER!

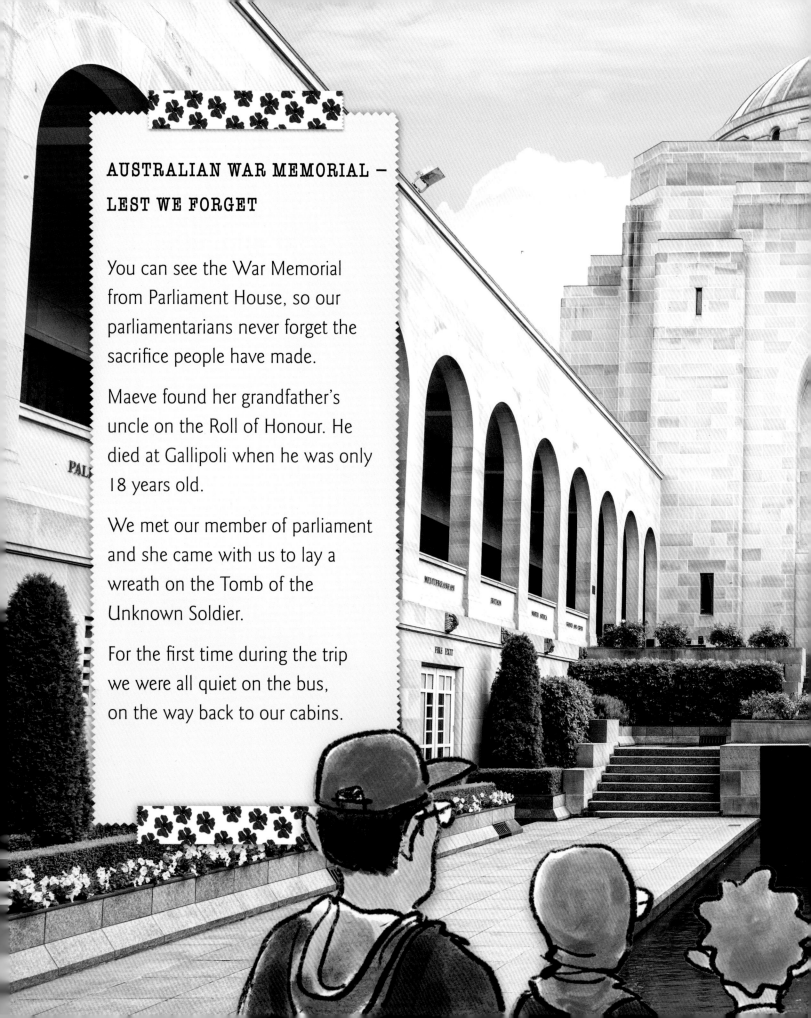

AUSTRALIAN WAR MEMORIAL – LEST WE FORGET

You can see the War Memorial from Parliament House, so our parliamentarians never forget the sacrifice people have made.

Maeve found her grandfather's uncle on the Roll of Honour. He died at Gallipoli when he was only 18 years old.

We met our member of parliament and she came with us to lay a wreath on the Tomb of the Unknown Soldier.

For the first time during the trip we were all quiet on the bus, on the way back to our cabins.

AIS
visitor centr
Training Centre
ised by the
ympic Committee

DAY 3   by the Holts

WINNING AT THE AUSTRALIAN
INSTITUTE OF SPORT (AIS)

When the bus pulled in to the AIS, we had our faces pressed up against the glass to see if we could spot a famous Olympian.

We tried different activities in the Sportex exhibition. Kira beat everyone – including our guide – at rowing, wheelchair racing and cycling.

The alpine racing machine was so much fun, we could feel the wind in our hair. Then we took a million selfies next to Cathy Freeman's running suits and shoes.

OUR MAIDEN SPEECHES AT THE MUSEUM OF AUSTRALIAN DEMOCRACY

The Museum of Australian Democracy is in Old Parliament House, and because it's an old building we had to wear white cotton gloves to protect it from damage.

We sat in the original Senate on the squishy leather chairs senators sat on years ago. The room smelled like varnished wood and my grandma's cupboards.

Some of us dressed up like famous politicians. I was Neville Bonner, the first Indigenous senator. Tilda was Dorothy Tangney, the first female senator. We both read speeches and wore funny outfits.

A COLLAGE OF
THE NATIONAL
PORTRAIT
GALLERY

LUNCH AT THE NATIONAL LIBRARY OF AUSTRALIA
BY MS SPARKS

Libraries are my favourite places in the world, and the National Library is my favourite of all. Aside from books, there are other treasures that tell stories in the gallery.

I took this photo of a lantern while the children were eating and asked them who it might have belonged to and why they needed it.

The Holts guessed:

• Diggers in the trenches in WW1 because they had no electricity. *Finn*

• In a house in the olden days so people could read before bedtime. *Taylor*

• Gold miners in their camps. *Jack*

ANSWER: It belonged to the bushranger Captain Moonlite, who would have used it for his last robbery.

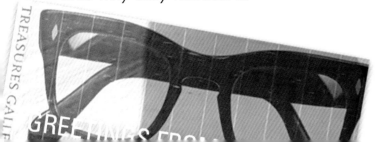

AUNTIE KAT AND THE ABORIGINAL TENT EMBASSY

When we left the Museum of Australian Democracy we met Alexandria's Auntie Kat just outside. She took us over the road to the Aboriginal Tent Embassy. The air was smoky from the ceremonial fire.

It's funny that democracy means 'people power' because not all the people get the power. When things aren't fair, people need to protest so that things can change.

Auntie Kat told us that the embassy was set up in 1972 to protest how Aboriginal people are treated in their own country. It has been there ever since. Auntie Kat said it's the longest protest in Australian history.
Before we left, Auntie Kat put some gum leaves on the fire for us and gave Alexandria a big hug.

Respect Aboriginal Rig

AWESOME EARTH

QUESTACON RULES!

Science is exciting, terrifying and fun all at the same time. There's always more to learn, create, experiment, wonder, fall into…

Somehow I survived a free fall, a lightning strike, an earthquake and my jumper that I'd been wearing for days!

I wasn't sick at all, except when I twisted my ankle and had a blood nose!

STAR GAZING AT THE MOUNT STROMLO OBSERVATORY

Mt Stromlo Observatory is the headquarters of the Australian National University's Research School of Astronomy and Astrophysics. It's filled with super-smart people.

Our guide was an astronomer who showed us a real meteorite and a Nobel Prize won by Professor Brian Schmidt (another super-smart person).

We gazed at stars through a serious telescope which made us feel super smart too. Maybe it's because we learnt so much about Australia, the universe and everything here in Canberra.

HOME AGAIN

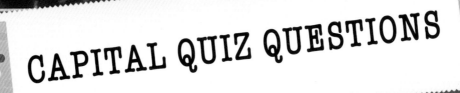

CAPITAL QUIZ QUESTIONS

Test yourself to see how much you know about Australia from your visit to Canberra.

1. What is the name of the prehistoric tree at the National Arboretum?

2. How long is Australian human history?

3. In what year did Federation take place?

4. Who represents the British Monarch in Australia?

5. What does the word 'Canberra' mean?

6. How old do you need to be to vote in Australian elections?

7. What are the two Houses of the Federal Parliament?

8. What is the name of the highest court?

9. Who was the first female Senator in the Federal Parliament?

10. What is Australia's longest running protest?

Answers

1. Wollemi Pine; 2. More than 65,000 years; 3. 1901; 4. The Governor-General; 5. 'Meeting Place'; 6. 18; 7. House of Representatives and the Senate; 8. The High Court; 9. Dorothy Tangney; 10. The Aboriginal Tent Embassy

To The
National
Institute of
Sport

Black
Mountain
Tower

BLACK MOUNT

To The
National
Arboretum

To Mount Stromlo
Observatory